James, Alexander and Lenny heard a long, plaintive scream, a flame-haired torpedo zipped over their heads and raced up the corridor.

'What was that?' shouted James, straightening his pointy wizard hat, which had been knocked sideways by the blast.

The smell that followed was inhuman: a rancid mix of fungus, rot, Camembert, unwashed hair, worms, burning plastic, sewage, BO, pig farms, mice and oranges that have been left in the bowl until their skins have turned green. There was only one place a smell like that could come from – and it was deep down, underneath the school.

The whirling, shrieking missile reached the door. Not pausing, even for a second, it vanished straight through it.

'Ah,' said Alexander. '*That* was what I was talking about.'

St Sebastian's School in Grimesford is the pits. No, really – it is.

Every year, the high school sinks a bit further into the boggy plague pit beneath it and, every year, the ghosts of the plague victims buried underneath it become a bit more cranky.

Egged on by their spooky ringleader, Edith Codd, they decide to get their own back – and they're willing to play dirty. *Really* dirty.

They kick up a stink by causing as much mischief as inhumanly possible so as to get St Sebastian's closed down once and for all.

But what they haven't reckoned on is year-seven new boy, James Simpson and his friends Alexander and Lenny.

The question is, are the gang up to the challenge of laying St Sebastian's paranormal problem to rest, or will their school remain forever frightful?

There's only one way to find out . . .

www.too-ghoul.com

B. STRANGE

EGMONT

Special thanks to:

**Serena Mackesy, St John's Walworth Church of
England Primary School and Belmont Primary School**

EGMONT
We bring stories to life

Which Witch? first published in Great Britain 2008
by Egmont UK Limited
239 Kensington High Street, London W8 6SA

Text & illustrations © 2008 Egmont UK Ltd
Text by Serena Mackesy
Illustrations by Pulsar Studios

ISBN 978 1 4052 3928 8

1 3 5 7 9 10 8 6 4 2

A CIP catalogue record for this title is available
from the British Library

Typeset by Avon DataSet Ltd, Bidford on Avon, Warwickshire
Printed and bound in Great Britain by the CPI Group

'Why has this series of books not won
The Grossest Thing in the World trophy???'

Anonymous, age 10

'Boys will love *Too Ghoul For School* cos
it's gruesome and disgusting!'

Joe, age 9

'So cool I can't stop reading'

Billy, age 11

'I think this series ROCKS!!!!!!!!
I thought it was awesome and funny, and I am
going to try to get the whole collection'

Ted, age 12

'I think these are the best books
I have ever read in my life'

Harry, age 9

We want to hear what *you* think about
Too Ghoul for School! Visit:

www.too-ghoul.com

for loads of cool stuff to do
and a whole lotta grot!

School versus...

Always gets top marks - for his ghost-busting skills!

James Simpson

Contender for the Nobel Prize - for shockingly poor gags

Alexander Tick

This is one boy whose eyes aren't bigger than his stomach...

Lenny Maxwell

. . . Ghoul!

Crone alert!
Approach this scabby
old spook with caution!

Edith Codd

Sees himself as
St Sebastian's secret
phantom pupil

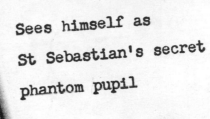

William Scroggins

This lazy, leech-
munching ghost just
longs to lounge in
peace . . .

Ambrose Harbottle

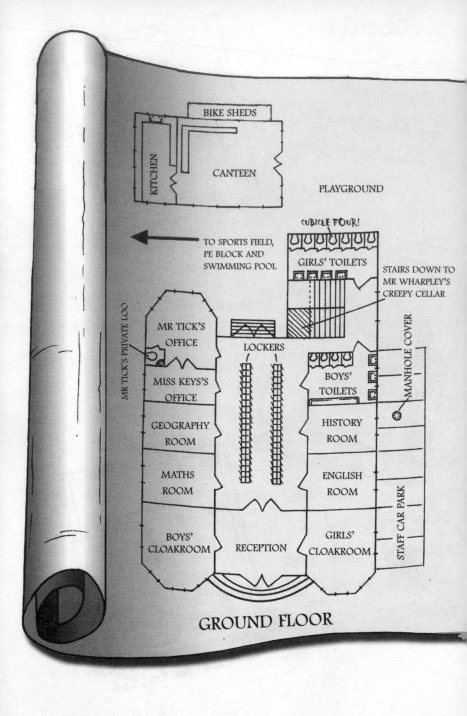

GROUND FLOOR

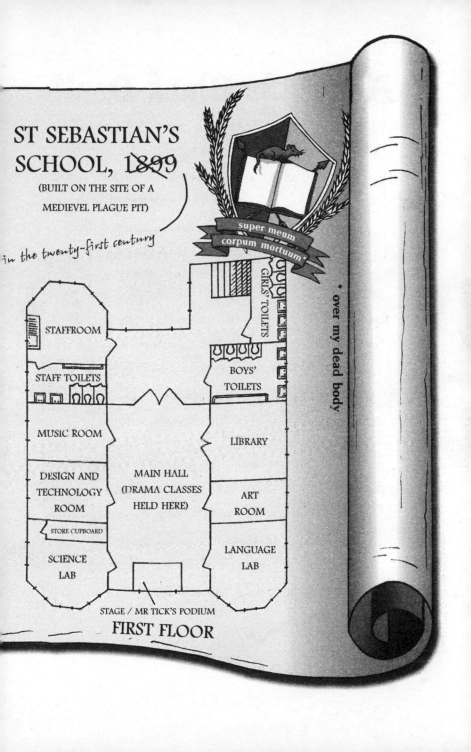

About the Black Death

The Black Death was a terrible plague that
is believed to have been spread by fleas on rats.
It swept through Europe in the fourteenth century,
arriving in England in 1348, where it killed
over one third of the population.

One of the Black Death's main symptoms was
**foul-smelling boils all over the body called
'buboes'.** The plague was so infectious that its
victims and their families were locked in their houses
until they died. Many villages were abandoned as
the disease wiped out their populations.

So many people died that graveyards overflowed
and bodies lay in the street, so special **'plague pits'**
were dug to bury the bodies. Almost every town
and village in England has a plague pit
somewhere underneath it, so watch out
when you're digging in the garden . . .

Dear Reader

As you may have already guessed, B. Strange is not a real name.

The author of this series is an ex-teacher who is currently employed by a little-known body called the Organisation For Spook Termination (Excluding Demons), or O.F.S.T.(E.D.). 'B. Strange' is the pen name chosen to protect his identity.

Together, we felt it was our duty to publish these books, in an attempt to save innocent lives. The stories are based on the author's experiences as an O.F.S.T.(E.D.) inspector in various schools over the past two decades.

Please read them carefully - you may regret it if you don't . . .

Yours sincerely
The Publisher.

PS - Should you wish to file a report on any suspicious supernatural occurrences at your school, visit **www.too-ghoul.com** and fill out the relevant form. We'll pass it on to O.F.S.T.(E.D.) for you.

PPS - All characters' names have been changed to protect the identity of the individuals. Any similarity to actual persons, living or undead, is purely coincidental.

CONTENTS

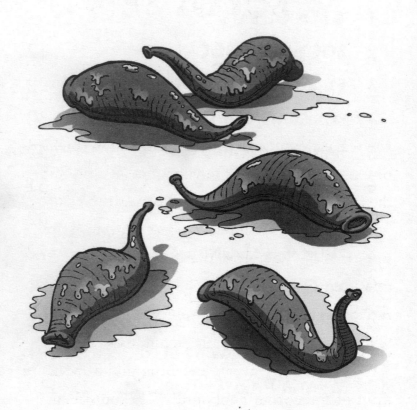

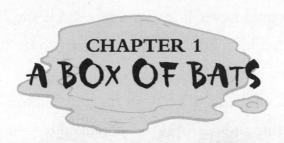

CHAPTER 1
A BOX OF BATS

Mr Wharpley dropped his noodle snack (pickled-onion-and-boiled-egg flavour) half-eaten on to the workbench and grumbled across the cellar.

'Blimmin' kids,' he muttered. A stray piece of slimy noodle flew from between his front teeth and landed in his moustache. 'Blimmin' Halloween. Ghouls and phantoms: they'll be telling me the magic pixies really exist next.'

Hands on hips, he surveyed the pile of boxes in front of the corner cupboard. The Halloween decorations were in there somewhere. He'd thrown them there himself just under a year ago.

'That pesky Miss Keys,' he grunted. 'I bet Mr Tick would never have remembered if she hadn't reminded him. Sticking her nose in where it's not wanted.'

He scratched the back of his head, behind his ear. A fine shower of dandruff sprinkled on to the shoulders of his brown caretaker's overall. 'I'm getting too old for this. Up and down ladders like a monkey, and what thanks do I get? Don't even get to finish my dinner in peace, that's what.'

Of all the events of the year, Mr Wharpley hated Halloween especially. Even more than Christmas. Even more than – he only just stopped himself spitting at the thought of all those pink tissue-paper hearts – Valentine's Day. Because the decorations for Halloween, more than any other day, need to be hung from ceilings. Plastic bats and cobwebs and witches' brooms and spiders: they just don't dangle the same way from a wall.

And ceilings meant ladders. And ladders meant only one thing to Mr Wharpley: danger. Because the only way to not get dizzy on a ladder is to not look down. And if you don't look down, you don't know what's beneath you. Which is asking for trouble.

The last time he'd been up a ladder had nearly been the end of him. His ears turned a strange shade of purple as he remembered: getting all the way to the second-from-top rung before he glanced down to see Gordon – a nasty piece of work, that Gordon, no wonder the kids called him 'The Gorilla' – running off with a pot of glue dangling from his meaty paws. It had taken half an hour of wobbly teetering to get his shoes untied and get free.

'I'm too old for this,' he repeated. He took one huge step over a nativity scene and one giant leap over a pile of Diwali lanterns. 'They should pay me danger money,' he groaned.

Mr Wharpley reached the cupboard, braced himself and pulled the door open. Twenty seconds later, when the shower of paper chains, fairy lights and rolled-up banners had slowed to the occasional bounce off the top of his head, he clapped eyes on the box he'd been looking for. It was easy to spot: there was a skeleton sticking out of the top.

Stacey and Leandra had their backs to the stairs, so they didn't see him approach. And James, Alexander and Lenny were too busy looking at Stacey to notice anything much. In fact, it was only when Mr Wharpley, his vision blocked by the box and its contents, bumped into Stacey that anyone noticed he was there at all.

Glow-in-the-dark skeletons, snaggle-toothed pumpkins, vampire bats and big hairy spiders cascaded from the open top. A bat landed in Stacey's hair. For a moment, everyone was transfixed. Then Stacey reached up and touched the bat's rubbery wings and let out a shriek that shocked them all into action.

'Get it off, get it off, getitooooffffff! Eeeeee!'
howled Stacey.

'Stay still!' shrieked Leandra. 'Don't move!'

James jumped forwards and helped her untangle
the bat's claws from her shiny blonde tresses.

'Aaaah, for the love of Elvis!' cursed Mr
Wharpley, as a tin of spray-on cobweb fell from
the box and rolled across the floor to come to a
halt by Lenny's foot. 'What are you lot doing
here?'

Lenny picked up the tin. 'It's lunch break, Mr
Wharpley,' he said helpfully. 'Can I give you a
hand?'

The back pocket of Mr Wharpley's overalls
started to hiss and crackle. 'Reg? Reg? Are you
there? Over.'

Glaring at Lenny, he dropped the box on the
floor and felt around his backside for the walkie-
talkie. 'Mr Wharpley here, over,' he said, pointedly.

'Ah, Reg,' said Miss Keys, not noticing. 'How

are you getting on with those decorations?'

Mr Wharpley snorted, making the piece of noodle wobble in his moustache like a wriggly worm. Stacey stopped shrieking to watch, fascinated.

'Yeah,' he said to Lenny, ignoring Miss Keys's plaintive tones, 'you can go and get the ladder and bring it to the hall for me, if you want to be helpful.'

Lenny lolloped off down the stairs on his size tens. The caretaker thumped his thumb down on the walkie-talkie button. 'Mr Wharpley here,' he barked. 'I'm on my way.'

'So,' said Leandra to the others as her brother shambled off, 'guess what?'

'What?' asked James.

'You know the Halloween disco?'

'You could hardly miss it,' replied James, 'it's all the year-seven girls have talked about for the last week. What about it?'

'Well, guess who's in charge?'

'Albert Einstein,' said Alexander.

They all looked at him. 'Who's Albert Einstein?' asked Stacey. 'Is he in your year?'

'No,' began Alexander, 'he's a famous physicist. He coined the Theory of Relativity, "e" equals "mc" squared, which is based around the concept that energy –'

'Naah!' gurned Leandra, ignoring him. 'Me and Stacey!'

'Stacey and I,' corrected Alexander.

'No, not you and Stacey – me and Stacey,' replied Leandra.

'No, no. I mean "Stacey and I" is right,' explained Alexander.

'Look, this is a disco, not Chess Club, Stick,' said Stacey. 'Why don't you leave it to us girls?

8

We know what we're doing.'

Alexander sighed heavily.

'Thing is . . .' began Leandra.

'Go on,' said Alexander.

'We've got to find some volunteers. Do you know anyone who can DJ? We don't know anyone.'

The words had left James's mouth before he could stop them. 'Sure,' he replied. 'That's no problem.'

He was rewarded with a dazzling smile. From Stacey – Leandra mercly rolled her eyes.

'Can you really?' asked Stacey.

'Course I can,' he heard himself saying. 'Piece of cake.'

'Did someone say cake?' said Lenny, reappearing just in time to hear the offer.

Alexander caught his friend's eye behind the girls' backs and gestured from James to Stacey. The penny dropped, and Lenny shared a secret

smirk with Alexander. James had never been near a turntable in his life. His urge to impress Stacey had got the better of him again.

'Great!' said Stacey. 'Cool! Thanks, James!'

'Any time,' he replied, confidently.

The three boys put their hands in their pockets and watched the girls walk off towards the playground, convinced they'd ticked off an item on their list.

'What on earth made you say that, James?' asked Lenny.

'He's always in a spin when Stacey's around,' said Alexander.

James glared. Lenny sniggered. 'Yeah,' he said. 'He gets all mixed up.'

Alexander sniggered back. 'Sorry, James. Just tune us out.'

'But seriously,' said Lenny, pulling himself together, 'how are you planning to get out of this one, James?'

James shrugged as Stacey and Leandra disappeared round the corner. 'I have absolutely no idea,' he said.

CHAPTER 2
BOOM-TCHKA-BOOM!

A few days later, William Scroggins, an eleven-year-old ghost (give or take a few hundred years), let himself slip quietly through the boiler-room drain, skirted the blubbery, rasping sound of Mr Wharpley's post-noodle afternoon nap and drifted up the school corridor.

William usually enjoyed his trips up through the sewer system to St Sebastian's. Having never gone to school when he was alive, he enjoyed pretending he was a pupil now he was dead. Today, though, he was less keen than usual.

Because today he was under orders, and being under orders from Edith Codd usually spelt trouble.

It had started three days before, when a strange new noise began to work its way down through the pipes and fill the ghosts' sewer home. Rhythmic, yet not. *Boom-tchka-boom!* it went, and *duh-m-duh-m-duh-m-boom!* over and over again, for an hour every lunchtime. The plague-pit bones rattled like ghastly wind chimes. Slugs lost their grip on the blackened ceilings and plopped on to the ghosts below. Lady Petronella Grimes had completely lost her head, and Ambrose had had quite a job to stick it back on.

William quite liked the sound, himself. It made him want to tap his feet. It had the opposite effect on Edith. Like many things to do with St Sebastian's, all it did was make her angry.

'Get up there!' she had shrieked at William, shaking her fist. So many flakes of ancient skin had flown from her fiery red hair that she had looked like she was in a snow-globe. 'And find out what's going on!'

He hadn't needed telling twice.

The school was empty. Most of the pupils were in the playground. A couple of year sevens were hiding in the boys' cloakroom, eating sherbet lemons. He could hear Miss Keys in her office, typing and talking on the phone.

'. . . Princess Pink,' she was saying, 'with green lapels. Do you think it would go with my yellow blouse? The one with the big bow on the front?'

The sound started up again. *Boom-tchka-boom-tchka-boom!* It was coming from upstairs. William, still none the wiser, drifted up them to investigate.

The noise was coming from the music room. The door juddered on its hinges. *Boom-tchka-boom!* it went.

What on earth is going on? thought William.

Have they got a marching band in there? A blacksmith?

Turning himself invisible, he went into the room. James, Alexander and Lenny were huddled around a table, frowning at a big silver box. The sound was so loud he couldn't hear himself haunt. Song sheets bounced on the music stands and even the boys' hair seemed to be jumping up and down with the rhythm.

The noise was coming from the box. William looked over their shoulders. It was shiny and covered in buttons and little red lights, which danced up and down in a line, in time with the beat of the music coming out of it. Looking more closely, he saw that there was a window on the front. And inside, a disc made of silver span round and round, so quickly you could barely see it!

William jumped backwards. His sunken blue eyes glowed in his face. 'Witchcraft!' he muttered.

The disc was moving of its own accord!

James pressed a button. The noise stopped, suddenly. The window opened and the disc popped out. William stared, mouth open, as James calmly picked it up. Why wasn't he afraid?

Alexander opened a small, flat box and produced another disc. 'Try this,' he said. James put it where the last disc had been and pressed another button.

Boom!

William jumped, startled. The box was making a new, different noise: more *doof-doof-doof-doof* than *boom-tchka-boom*. The three year sevens broke into wide smiles and nodded at each other in time with the noise. *Is it music?* wondered William. Was that what it was?

Lenny shouted something.

'What?' bellowed James.

He tried again.

'What?' shouted James.

He pressed the 'off' button just as Lenny had another try.

'I SAID, ARE YOU EXCITED ABOUT DJ-ING?' he yelled into the silence.

The three boys fell about. William laughed so much he almost became visible, but caught himself just in time. Though not before a whiff of rotten eggs escaped his spectral form.

'More nervous than excited, to be honest,' replied James.

'Oh, so *that's* what that smell is,' said Lenny.

'Wasn't me,' said James.

William felt guilty. He knew only too well what the stink was. Being a sewer-pit ghost had serious drawbacks.

'Must've been Alexander,' said Lenny.

'I endeavour not to flatulate in company,' said Alexander.

'Flatulate? What on earth is that?'

'A verb,' began Alexander, 'derived from

flatulence, which is —'

'Never mind,' said Lenny, pulling out another silver disc. 'How about this one, James?'

James pressed a button and the noise started again. *Mmm-pa-mmm-pa-mmm-pa-mmm-pa.*

As he watched the boys smile once more and start nodding along with the rhythm, William

noticed something weird. His foot, without any permission from himself, had started tapping. He looked down and was even more surprised to find that his leg had followed suit. Before he knew what was happening, the other leg had joined in, kicking heel-to-toe in time with the music. Amazed, he watched as both hands began to wave in the air, back and forth.

He was dancing!

Well, it can't be black *magic*, he thought as he jigged off. *Nothing this fun can be bad.*

He continued to jig as he followed the corridor on his way to report back to Edith. Though what he was going to tell her about this strange, exciting development, he wasn't sure. As he passed the noticeboard at the bottom of the stairs, something caught his eye. He stopped, jigged backwards and stood still to study it more closely.

It was a poster. Striking colours – black and

red – and big letters, and pictures of the shiny magic discs. Another of a boy spinning them, just as James had been doing. And all over the poster, something that made his heart leap. Ghosts! Dancing ghosts! As clear as day and twice as spooky!

William couldn't read, but it wasn't difficult for him to tell what the poster meant. It was easy! St Sebastian's wanted to make friends with them! They were throwing a ball, the plague-pit ghosts were invited, and there would be dancing!

He grinned from ear to ear. He pictured himself 'hanging out' with the 'friends' he'd never actually spoken to: James, Alexander, Lenny – even Stacey, with her blonde hair and her wide blue eyes – jigging about with him in a circle. A party!

Carefully, he pulled down the poster, rolled it up and headed for the sewer. Lady Grimes, or one of the other ghosts, would be able to read it properly, and tell him the details.

CHAPTER 3
THINK I'LL GO AND EAT WORMS

'What did you do with the eyeballs, Lynn?' asked Mrs Meadows.

'They're in the jar next to the worms,' replied Mrs Cooper. 'I presume we're not doing anything about the brains until the last minute?'

'No,' said Mrs Meadows. 'We wouldn't want the toast to go soggy.'

It was the day before the disco, and the dinner ladies were bustling about preparing Halloween snacks.

'How about those fingernails?' asked Mrs

Meadows, her head buried deep in the vegetable fridge, where she was looking for the ketchup to make blood to go on the cheesy vampire fangs.

Mrs Cooper snatched the opportunity to help herself to a handful of worms. She couldn't help it. She loved those chewy jelly sweets almost as much as she loved a nice cup of tea and a biscuit. They were just so . . . *fruity*, she thought. There was an entire sweet-shop-sized jar sitting beside the jar of gobstopper eyeballs, waiting to go into the green jelly, and she couldn't resist.

'All done,' she said, 'and on the middle shelf of the meat fridge.'

She quickly popped the sweets into her mouth and, chewing like a cow, bustled off to check that there were enough tins of spaghetti to make the 'brains on toast' for tomorrow. Mrs Meadows emerged triumphant from the fridge, brandishing a bottle. 'I still think,' she said, 'we should have done those phantom moulds.'

Mrs Cooper swallowed the last of her mouthful of sweets before she came out from behind her own door.

'We can't make them eat blancmange at dinnertime, Sue,' she reminded her. 'What makes you think they'd eat it at a party?'

Mrs Meadows put the bottle down and took a moment to tidy her stringy hair back under her net hat.

'Well, nobody seems to think they'll have a problem eating tombstones,' she said.

The worms were just too tempting. Mrs Cooper squeezed her ample bottom through the gap between the fridge and the stainless-steel counter and surreptitiously went over to stand beside the jar.

'Yes, but *they're* only chocolate biscuits,' she said, 'shaped to *look* like tombstones. How many bottles of blood have we got?' she asked, knowing that Mrs Meadows would have to pop into the pantry to find out the answer.

Her hand shot into the worm jar as soon as Mrs Meadows turned her back. She grabbed four, five, in a single scoop and stuffed them into her mouth.

'Plenty,' Mrs Meadows informed her, returning. 'We've got eight big bottles of blackcurrant cordial. That should make enough blood to go round, shouldn't it?'

'Mfff,' said Mrs Cooper, her mouth occupied with chewing, 'mi food fink fo.'

'Hello,' said a voice she hadn't been expecting from just beside her left shoulder.

Mrs Cooper breathed in the last of her worms in surprise and started coughing. The worms went so far down the wrong way that she wasn't sure if they weren't going to come out the other end. Alternately coughing and hiccuping, she had to hold on to the counter to stop herself falling over altogether.

She was saved by Sue Meadows, who dealt her
a sharp blow between her shoulder blades. A bit
sharper, she thought later, than strictly necessary,
if the look on Mrs Meadow's face was anything
to go by. Whatever, it did the trick, because a
plug of jelly shot from her mouth and skidded
across the floor, where it came to rest stickily
against the fire extinguisher.

'Hello, Leandra, hello, Stacey,' said Mrs
Meadows, pointedly reaching behind Mrs
Cooper and screwing the lid back on the jar of
worms.

The owner of the voice swam into Mrs
Cooper's vision. It was Leandra Maxwell, with
her friend Stacey Carmichael two steps behind.
Stacey seemed to be examining her reflection in
the polished steel doors of the big bank of ovens.

Mrs Cooper dabbed her watering eyes. 'What
can we do for you, girls?'

'We were wondering how the preparations
were going for tomorrow night,' Leandra said
importantly.

Mrs Cooper still wasn't quite right. While Mrs
Meadows banged her back once more, she
nodded and pointed to the fridge. Leandra and
Stacey went and opened it.

'Eeeee!' shrieked Stacey, jumping back
theatrically.

'What?' cried Mrs Meadows.

'Fingers! There's a tray of severed fingers in there!'

Mrs Cooper was delighted. She'd spent an hour creating them out of cocktail sausages, and it was nice to see that they were convincing. She had made 'fingernails' out of slivers of hard cheese, and attached them with gobs of cream cheese. And jolly effective they looked too, she thought: the cheese squeezing round the edges of the nails looked rather like pus. And from what she remembered from her own school days, the bubonic plague had involved plenty of pus.

'Don't be silly, Stacey,' said Leandra. 'Don't you remember the bubonic fingers?'

'Oh, yes,' said Stacey, fanning herself. 'Very realistic.

'This is going to be the best party *ever!*' announced Leandra as she supported a wobbly Stacey through the canteen.

'If I ever recover,' replied Stacey. She was still a little bit green after her shock.

As they came out into the playground, they bumped into Alexander, who had been checking the rainfall meter he had fixed to the beam of the bike sheds. Alexander frowned as he caught sight of Stacey.

'Are you all right, Stacey?' he asked.

'Oh, don't worry about her,' said Leandra. 'She's just been in the school kitchen.'

'Oh, dear,' said Alexander understandingly. 'Not steak and kidney *again*?'

Leandra shook her head. 'No, she saw the snacks the dinner ladies are doing for the disco and they made her come over a bit weird.'

'I'm not surprised,' joked Alexander. 'It must have been a dream come true for them – making food that's *meant* to make you feel sick!'

Leandra laughed.

'Anyway,' said Alexander, 'you're not the only one who's feeling sick, Stacey. James is going green every five minutes.'

'Why? What's he got to be nervous about?' asked Leandra. 'He's only playing tunes.'

'Well, yes,' said Alexander, 'but given that it's

the first time he's —' He stopped short. 'Um,' he said.

'What are you talking about?' asked Leandra, glowering.

'Um, nothing,' he said. 'I was just . . . um, he's looking forward to it immensely . . . I mean . . .'

'Alexander,' Leandra's voice had a dangerous edge of something dark and scary to it, 'are you telling me James doesn't know what he's doing?'

'No, no,' floundered Alexander. 'It's all under control, don't worry. Everything's . . .'

He never got to finish his sentence because Leandra had stamped off in the direction of the main school building, her face like thunder.

Stacey shrugged her shoulders and trailed in her wake, wondering if there was a chance she might get a sit-down with a nice magazine to recover from her shock.

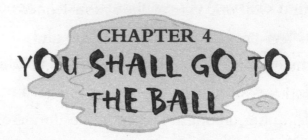

CHAPTER 4
YOU SHALL GO TO THE BALL

One of the drawbacks of being a self-appointed leader is that your followers sometimes don't, well, follow you. Edith Codd often had this problem. Her fellow plague-pit ghosts seemed to carry on as though she had never taken charge half the time, deciding to do things without her permission, going about the place as though they were free to do so, forgetting to tell her things. Sometimes, she suspected, they even did it on purpose!

This was why she had had to take up spying.

Earwigging, she liked to call it, in honour of the time when she had had her face pressed to a hole in a wall and one of the many-legged insects had crawled out of the sludge and straight into her ear. As far as she knew, it was still in there. Sometimes she could feel it wriggling about.

It was through earwigging that she found out about the ball. That wretched boy, William Scroggins, had been under strict instructions to find out what the dreadful thumping noise coming from above ground was and report back to her, but he'd done nothing of the sort! Instead, he'd gone straight to Lady Petronella Grimes, carrying a large sheet of rolled-up paper under his scrawny arm, and had been there ever since. Did he think she wouldn't notice? Edith Codd noticed everything!

She didn't, however, notice the drip-drip-drip of mucus from the big batch of fungi growing on the pillar she was hiding behind. She was too caught up in listening to the conversation going on on the other side. The mucus absorbed into her hair, giving a sticky, silvery sheen to its normal blazing red. An unlucky beetle blundered into it in the dark and stayed there, struggling as though caught in quicksand, and she didn't notice. The news was all too fascinating.

'Go on,' said William. 'Read it again. Just one more time!'

Lady Grimes sighed, but indulged him. She didn't mind. She was quite excited herself by the news he had brought.

'*Are you in high spirits about Halloween?*' she read. '*Then you'll love St Sebastian's "Halloween Hell-raiser"!*

Feast on foul and fiendish finger food then rattle your

bones to haunting melodies from DJ Death (also known as James Simpson).

This Friday evening in the main hall from five till eight. Dress grim and ghastly.

Come one, come all, to the ghoulish ball!'

They had gathered a crowd of ghosts around them as William insisted on hearing the content of the poster over and over again. Ambrose Harbottle leant on the other side of Edith's pillar, plucking leeches from his pocket and chewing distractedly on them while he took in this development.

'You see?' cried William. 'They want us!'

'It certainly seems so,' said Lady Grimes. 'Ah, such a long time since I danced! What fun we shall have!'

The Headless Horseman, seated on a pile of bones, picked up a nearby skull and nodded it in agreement. Bertram ran off a scale on his ribcage xylophone. The notes rattled around the

ceiling and bounced back eerily. 'Perhaps,' he
suggested, 'we should think about bringing them
something in return. Some music, perhaps? I
don't know what a DJ can be, but he'll get very
tired playing his instrument all alone for the
entire evening. What do you say, band?'

The Plague Pit Junior Ghost Band raised a
ghastly clatter of bones and a chorus of
agreement. Bertram had recently invented the
knuckle-bone flute, which had proved to be a hit
among his young followers.

'It is so very, very kind,' said Lady Grimes,
fanning herself with a surprised bat that she had
plucked from his perch on the ceiling. 'To think
of us on our special night.'

Edith snorted so loudly at this that she almost
gave herself away in her hiding place. The
wimps! Any opportunity to be suckered and they
would take it!

'Didn't I tell you?' asked William. 'I knew that

if we just gave them a chance they would want to make friends!'

William had always been a hopeful child when he was alive, and he was no different in death. Plus, he had spent enough time observing James, Alexander, Stacey, Leandra and Lenny to know that any party they were involved with would be fun.

'Mmm,' said Ambrose. 'I'm dying to know about this so-called "finger food". Do you think it might actually be made of fingers?'

Absent-mindedly, as he imagined the delights in store, he dug a finger of his own deep into his left nostril. After a long excavation, he withdrew the digit to find a trail of slimy brain had attached itself to his fingernail. 'Mmm,' he said, popping the delicacy between his lips and giving it a good, sucky chew. 'Better, perhaps, with a little toast . . .'

'What to wear?' Lady Grimes asked the

stench-filled air. 'It's so long since I was in
society, I'm sure I have no idea of the latest
modes.'

'You will look beautiful whatever you wear,
my dear,' said Ambrose nobly, and swallowed
another bit of his brain.

Edith crept away, frothing slightly at one corner
of her mouth. The fools! Thinking they could
keep this from her! And even more foolish – the
mortals in the world above! It seemed as though,
for once, William Scroggins was right. Well, even
a little idiot like Scroggins could get it right
sometimes. These people actually thought they
could make up for years of torture with some
jigging and a plate of eyeballs!

She muttered as she swept through the sewer's
echoing chambers.

'As if! As if they can buy off a ghost with a "haunting melody"! The cheek of it! I'll give them "haunting"! They'll be so haunted their hair will stand on end permanently!'

Still, she reflected, they clearly knew very little about ghosts, if the poster was anything to go by. The pictures were nothing more than sheets with eyeholes cut in them! Ridiculous! If they had ever seen a real ghost, such as herself, they'd get the shock of their lives.

'Yes, but,' she muttered, 'ignorance is bliss. Bliss for me, anyway! An expert planner like me will have a whale of a time!'

Curse that Scroggins boy, she thought. Withholding information again, as though it would stop her! True, a little more time to prepare would have given her a chance to be *really* inventive, but nothing would stop her from taking the opportunity in front of her.

'Hah!' she cackled. 'And I won't even have to

bother with a disguise! Dress grim and ghastly? I'll come as myself!'

Edith Codd headed in the direction of the sewer leading to the boys' toilets. She'd give them a ball to remember! Oh, yes, she would!

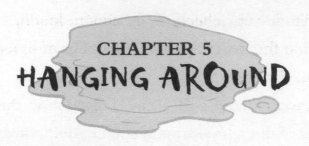

CHAPTER 5
HANGING AROUND

Leandra felt important carrying a clipboard. *A clipboard is like having a big sign round your neck saying I'm in charge,* she thought. She ignored her brother and his friends over by the DJ's area as she and Stacey marched about the hall.

Everybody had done exactly as she had said, and the hall looked perfect. With the help of Mr Wharpley and his rusty staple gun, it had been transformed into a convincing Dracula castle, festooned with cobwebs and bats and skeletons and even a very realistic creepy old witch, who dangled from the ceiling, grinning. She looked as though she might move at any moment.

'Plastic cups, check,' said Leandra loudly, ticking the items off on her list, 'jugs of blood, check, bubonic fingers, check.'

Stacey caught sight of her reflection in the glass of the school trophy cabinet and adjusted her witch's hat. She and Leandra had spent a lot of time on their costumes, and they were pleased with the results. Though secretly Stacey wished she had made her dress a bit shorter; she'd already picked up a fine collection of dust and hair from the floor. 'Check,' she said.

'Fancy-dress prize,' said Leandra.

'Check,' said Stacey, ticking off the big bag of Halloween candy.

'Eyeball jelly, check,' said Leandra.

'Check,' said Stacey. The spiders looked very realistic. She was slightly nervous that they might not all be made of rubber.

'Tell me again,' said James to Lenny, 'why your sister's dressed as a cat.'

'She's a *black* cat,' said Lenny. 'Black cats go with witches, don't they.'

'Actually, they're called familiars,' interrupted Alexander.

'Well, of course Leandra and Stacey are familiar,' replied Lenny, nonplussed, 'they're best friends.'

'Yeah,' agreed James. He turned to Lenny. 'I mean, they don't exactly look ghoulish, do they?'

'That's girls for you,' said Lenny, who was dressed as a zombie, and rolled his eyes.

Alexander sighed. He crawled under the table to plug in the CD player while Lenny busily laid out the music selection on the table. James looked on nervously and stroked his beard. He was glad, now, that he'd come as a wizard, as the costume covered most of his face. He'd spent every spare minute of the previous week practising his DJ-ing skills, but he still felt nervous.

'As for you, Alexander,' said Lenny, 'are you wearing leggings?'

Alexander nodded. 'I borrowed them from my mother's gym bag.'

'Why?' asked Lenny.

'I'm a fourteenth-century ghost and it's in keeping with the period,' said Alexander. 'It's a tribute to the historical roots of the school. A tunic and leggings was the standard mode of dress for a medieval peasant. As were clogs.'

'Yes,' said Lenny, 'but I don't suppose their clogs were made of red plastic.'

'Yes,' said Alexander, 'well, you're not allowed wooden clogs in the gym. Besides, they would have very little traction on an exercise bicycle. Wood is . . .'

'Yes,' said Lenny, but he wasn't really listening

as he'd noticed that James had turned pale.
'James,' he said, grabbing the nearest plate, 'have
some brains on toast!'

James went from white to green.

'Give me those!' said Leandra, whipping the
plate from his hand. 'You can't hog the brains.
They're for later.'

'I'm only doing what the undead do,' protested
Lenny. 'I'm a zombie, remember?'

'A blithering idiot, more like,' returned his sister, shooting him a look.

'All right?' asked Elvis. Mr Wharpley never let a chance to wear his Elvis costume pass him by, even if it was Halloween.

'It's amazing, Mr Wharpley,' replied Stacey, eyeing the bats to check that they weren't going to come alive and get into her hair again. 'I can't believe what you've managed to do. It's all so . . . realistic.'

'All in a day's work,' puffed Mr Wharpley.

'The centrepiece is especially good,' said Stacey. 'You would almost think it was about to fly down from the ceiling.'

Mr Wharpley squinted up through his thick black quiff at the witch on the ceiling. Bright carroty hair she had, and greenish skin covered in flaky boils, and a mouthful of teeth that looked like they had been fished out of a dustbin and put in without being washed. *Funny*, he thought, *you'd think I'd remember putting that up there. She's as ugly as a box of bats.*

A flake broke loose from the boil on the witch's nose and drifted lazily down towards him. 'Yes, well,' he said, 'if a professional caretaker can't put on a good show for Halloween, he doesn't deserve to call himself a . . .'

Stacey was no longer listening. No one was listening, in fact. James, Alexander and Lenny were all staring up at the hideous crone on the ceiling.

'You know what this means, don't you?' asked James.

'Are you thinking what I'm thinking?' asked Lenny.

'I think I am,' said Alexander.

'What are we going to −' began James, but broke off when, with a bang, the hall doors flew back and in stalked − all three boys felt their eyes swivel back, forth and back again − the exact same witch! Same red hair, same red eyes, same pitted skin, same hideous grin.

'What the −' began Alexander.

'It was the last costume in the shop, OK?' came a man's voice.

'D–dad – Mr Tick?' asked Alexander.

'I don't want to hear another word,' said Mr Tick.

Miss Keys, who had just poured herself a cup of blood, began to titter. Her vampire fangs shot out of her mouth and landed on the floor.

CHAPTER 6
BANGING TUNES

'What do you think she's going to do?' asked Alexander.

The witch — the one who wasn't a headmaster — was doing a lot of nothing at the moment, though her eyes swivelled like marbles in her head.

'A bit of haunting would be my first guess,' James said sarcastically.

'Followed by a bit of haunting?' joined in Lenny.

'Yes, thank you very much,' said Alexander,

'I think I had worked that much out for myself.'

'Is she one of the ones from the plague pit?' asked Lenny.

'Undoubtedly,' said Alexander. 'All of the manifestations at St Sebastian's have been, in my experience, related to that particular architectural feature.'

Lenny looked at him blankly. 'The real question is,' he asked, 'not what she's going to do, but what we're going to do about it.'

'Wait and see?' asked James.

'Yes,' said Alexander. 'It's possible she's merely on a surveillance mission.'

'Or finding out how to teach you to speak English, perhaps,' muttered Lenny.

'Yes,' said James, 'and frankly I've got more pressing things to worry about. Like the fact that the guests are arriving and I haven't even got a disc in the player.'

Stacey stood at the door, beaming. Judging by the number of guests streaming past, her and Leandra's hard work had been a huge success. The turnout, and the costumes, were fantastic!

Perhaps if Stacey had been a bit more observant, she would have noticed just how fantastic the turnout was. Because many of the costumes were not costumes at all. The ghosts, who believed that they were the guests of honour, were, of course, coming through the front door, happily mingling with the vampires, zombies, mummies and witches of St Sebastian's School. All of them, from the biggest to the smallest, had practised staying visible in readiness for this special occasion.

'Wow,' said Stacey to a headless corpse who strode past with a skull beneath its arm, 'that must have taken you hours!'

The Headless Horseman bowed deeply and passed into the hall. He was followed by Bertram and the Plague Pit Junior Ghost Band.

A slightly whiffy figure paused and turned black-ringed eyes on her. He was too tall to be a pupil, but his flaky, pale make-up was so thick she couldn't tell which teacher he was. *Mr Parker?*

she wondered. *No. His ears are too small. Mr Drew?*
Mr Downe?

The figure bowed deeply and brandished a
glass jar. 'Just a humble gesture, my dear,' he said.

'Thank you,' said Stacey. She liked presents.
The jar's contents were pale, slithery and floated
in brackish water. 'What are those?'

'Just a little snack for later,' replied Ambrose
Harbottle, the leech merchant. 'Harvested fresh
this morning.'

Stacey put the jar carefully on the table beside
her. Some people were taking this costume thing
a bit too far.

James had been nervous enough as it was. Now
that he was watching a mass of vampires,
werewolves, headless corpses and teachers
attempting to dance while the sewer witch
dangled over their heads, he could hardly stop his

hands shaking long enough to hit a button. In fact, he had hit so many wrong buttons he barely remembered which ones were the right ones.

The track was coming to an end. He would need to change over in twenty seconds. He hadn't yet put the next CD in the slot. Sweating, he fumbled it from its case and pressed the 'open' button.

The speakers fell silent. He'd opened the drawer for the CD that was still playing.

'Oh, poo,' whispered James. Ghosts, wizards, zombies and vampires stopped dancing and stood there staring at him. He waved, trying to look cheery. 'All under control!' he called, swapped the discs over and hit 'play'. Skeletons, mummies, Frankenstein's monster and Elvis began to shuffle about again. James wiped his forehead on the sleeve of his wizard costume.

Please, he thought, *please don't let that witch decide to do anything. This night can't get any worse.*

Leandra Maxwell pushed through the crowd and stood in front of the DJ's table. She put clenched fists on her hips and glared.

Lenny, on the other side of the room, saw her arrive. *Uh-oh*, he thought. *Here comes trouble.* He quickly filled a cup with blood and began to work his way towards his friend and his angry sister.

'You need to sort yourself out, James!' hissed Leandra. 'You're ruining the whole evening!'

'Steady on,' said James. 'People are enjoying themselves, aren't they?'

Leandra started wagging a finger. This was a bad sign. A very, very bad sign. 'They *may* be enjoying themselves, James Simpson,' hissed Leandra, 'but it's no thanks to you!'

57

William was having a rather nice chat with Stacey. She thought he was Alexander in disguise, but he didn't mind. Now that the school had made peace with the ghosts, there would be plenty of time for everyone to sort out who was who.

'So, she made her ears out of old egg boxes and velvet,' Stacey was saying, 'and then glued them on to a hairband.'

'That's very clever,' said William, having no idea whatsoever what egg boxes were. He could see that James was in trouble with Leandra. Her finger-wagging had turned into full-on arm-waving. *Poor old James*, he thought. *That Leandra scares* me, *and I've been dead for four hundred years*. He was relieved to see that Lenny had almost reached them, carrying a glass of the drink they were calling blood.

'Your boils are very realistic,' said Stacey. 'What did you use? Salad cream?'

'Oh, no,' said William, not really understanding the question, 'would that have helped, do you think?'

Lenny was coming up behind Leandra. James was practically backing away from the table to get out of range of her flailing hands. The Headless Horseman was jiving with Ms Legg, the PE teacher. Ambrose and Lady Grimes were waltzing. The Plague Pit Junior Ghost Band had formed a circle with a group of year sevens, and each was taking it in turns to jump into the middle and break-dance. One of them lost a forearm, but grabbed it with the other hand and waved it around his head. Everybody clapped, impressed.

Something suddenly made William look upwards. If he'd been able, he would have felt a chill all the way down his spine. Because, hanging from the ceiling, warts and all, was Edith Codd: large as life and twice as ugly.

'Oh, *no!*' he said, out loud.

'What?' asked Stacey.

William hurriedly pointed over to the DJ table. 'Looks like Leandra's on the warpath,' he said.

'Mmm,' said Stacey. 'Perhaps I should go over.'

Lenny's hand, with the cup of blood, was caught by Leandra's waving arm. The cup flew

through the air as if in slow motion, bounced and landed upside-down on the CD player. With a shriek and a shower of sparks, the player stopped. The hall fell silent. The dancers, groaning, all looked over at James.

William looked up again. Edith grinned a black and ghastly grin, drew a finger across her throat, then pressed it to her skinny lips.

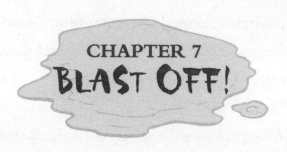

CHAPTER 7
BLAST OFF!

Edith didn't wait long. In fact, she didn't wait at all. There was nothing she enjoyed more than a good set-to with the living. Party? She'd give them a party!

She launched herself from the ceiling.

'Oh, crikey,' said Alexander, looking up from the smoking CD player, 'we're in for it now.'

'Too right you are!' yelled Leandra. 'That's my dad's CD player! Do you know how much it cost?'

'No,' corrected Alexander, pointing upwards, 'I mean we're *really* in for it now.'

The witch swooped, dress flapping, hands like claws, eyes glowing red with fury and glee. Mr Wharpley's black wig flew from his head with a single swipe; his comb-over followed halfway, and stayed there, sticking up from his head like a punk's Mohican.

Miss Keys dropped her vampire teeth again. What on earth was Mr Tick up to? The last time she'd seen him, he had had a cup of blood in one hand and a bubonic finger in the other. Had someone slipped something in his drink?

She watched as the witch whirled through the crowd, slashing, biting, clawing and shrieking.

'Headmaster!' she cried.

'Yaaa-ha-ha-ha-haaaa!' cackled the witch from the ceiling. 'Trick or treat!'

64

James, Alexander and Lenny froze as the air filled with flying feathers, bandages, bits of cape and airborne neck-bolts. 'Take that!' shrieked the crazy old witch, swiping at a passing werewolf. 'Happy Halloween!'

'Oh, crikey,' said Alexander again.

The disco was a scene of chaos. Pupils and teachers alike covered their heads and bolted for the exit, tripping each other up as they ran. Leandra's cat tail was ripped from the back of her leotard. Madame Dupont, looking surprisingly elegant while dressed as a knight, had her sword ripped from her hands and buried in the head of her dancing partner. Fortunately, her dancing partner was a ghost. He pulled the sword from his skull and offered it gallantly back to her.

Madame Dupont screamed and followed the crowd.

A group of year sevens linked arms to make a

circle, back to back, and started to work their way towards the fire exit. This would have been a good plan if the attack had been coming from the ground – from rats, for instance – so they could kick it away, but, as it was coming from the air, all it did was tie their arms up so they couldn't defend themselves. Every one was nursing a slashed ear in seconds.

The hag rose up in the air and surveyed the mayhem below. Enraged, she shook her fist at her ghostly troops, who seemed not to have noticed her presence at all. 'Traitors!' she shrieked. 'Turncoats! Connivers!'

'Seems like something's getting her goat,' said Lenny.

'You don't say,' said James.

The witch swooped down once more, scattering year eights before her like ball-bearings. Mr Wharpley, face covered in green jelly, crashed into the table, knocking it flying.

Without their shield, James, Alexander and Lenny found themselves caught up by the surge of the crowd. Before they knew it, they were being carried through the doors into the corridor.

'Have some leech wine,' said Ambrose.

'Don't mind if I do,' said Aggie Malkin. 'Good party, would you say?'

'Indeed,' said Ambrose. 'Lively, certainly.'

'How things have changed since my day,' observed Lady Petronella Grimes. 'I can't think what my husband would have made of such a display. He used to become enraged if he witnessed so much as an over-lively jig. And I'm not sure what to make of their music. It does seem to start and stop rather, doesn't it?'

'Times change, my dear,' replied Ambrose. 'And we must change with them. Do you think this is a new tradition? This ungainly rush for the doors?'

'I'm not sure,' said Bertram. 'Oh, look! William seems to have joined in. There he is, halfway into the corridor. And he seems to be waving!'

They all waved back. 'I'm sure he'll tell us what it was all about later,' said Lady Grimes.

'Speaking of music,' said Bertram, signalling to his band, 'how about a tune of our own?'

The Plague Pit Junior Ghost Band raised their instruments and set up an eerie drone.

They had been carried by the crowd most of the way down the corridor before James finally managed to grab Alexander and Lenny and pull them over to the side.

'We've got to stop her!' he cried. 'This is bedlam!'

They all stopped to look at the witch, who stood in the middle of the crowd, panting. She looked large, red and very evil.

'Yes, but how?' asked Lenny.

Alexander thought. 'We must create a diversion,' he suggested. 'Draw her off.'

'Of course,' said Lenny sarcastically. 'And get slashed ourselves.'

'No,' said James, 'Alexander's right. If we lure her to Mr Wharpley's cellar, we could get her down that drain and back into the sewer. Good thinking, Alexander!'

He stepped forwards and started waving his arms. 'Oi! Grandma! Call that a costume?'

Lenny joined in. He hooked his little fingers into the corners of his mouth, showing his teeth, and pressed his nose into a piggy snout. 'Seen yourself in a mirror lately?'

'Course she hasn't!' shouted James. 'Cos it would have cracked!'

The hag came to a halt, turned and looked at them.

'That's the sort of face only a mother could love!' shouted Alexander.

The witch hitched up her skirts to show a pair of hairy legs topped off with brown suede brogues and Prince-of-Wales check golfing socks. She took a step towards them.

'Love the fashion sense!' shouted James. 'What did you do, get dressed in the dark?'

'Whoops,' said Alexander. 'That one seemed to do the trick.'

They belted down the stairs. The witch was hot on their heels: they could hear her ghastly panting and smell her hideous breath. 'James Simpson!' she croaked. 'Come here immediately!'

They skidded, wheeled and ran on, clattering down the steps to the cellar. It was dark. The smell of damp and noodle snacks filled their noses. The witch was gaining on them. Alexander shuddered as her fingers brushed the back of his neck and an angry voice called his name.

The doorway loomed up, dark and empty. As they reached it, each boy jumped aside. The witch, however, couldn't stop. She shot past, and they heard a crash as she discovered Mr Wharpley's collection of buckets.

James reached out and slammed the door and Alexander turned the key. The three of them leant against it, panting heavily.

'That was a bit too close for my liking,' said Lenny.

'You can say that again,' said James.

Inside, a thunder of hammering and shouting started up.

'Boys!' shouted the witch. 'Boys, let me out RIGHT NOW! Lenny, James, Alexander! Open this door!'

Faintly, behind the voice, they could hear the strains of Elvis Presley. Mr Wharpley must have left a CD playing on loop as he dressed for the party.

CHAPTER 8
EDITH IS A LOONY

Miss Keys had taken her vampire teeth out altogether and hung them from a coat hook. She stood determinedly, stopping people from going into the cloakrooms: it was up to her, she had decided, to take charge. All she knew was that she had to protect the school and, most importantly, protect Mr Tick.

William, fighting his way back towards the hall, found her blocking the way. 'No, no, you can't go,' she was saying to anyone who would listen. 'It's a joke, that's all. A Halloween prank.'

Mr Watts, who had come dressed as a star-ship captain, brandished the torn sleeve of his nylon uniform.

'Call this a prank?' he asked, heatedly.

'Perhaps it did go a little far,' said Miss Keys. 'Mr Tick's been under a lot of strain, you know: inspectors; builders; all those problems with the toilets. People don't seem to understand what a responsibility being a headmaster is . . .'

Leandra and Stacey, meanwhile, were determined that nothing – not even a witch attack – was going to spoil their party. They had rushed over to the canteen and made up a new supply of blood, which they were pressing into people's hands.

'We hope you liked our floor-show,' Leandra chirped. She forced herself to wink. 'Bet you didn't expect that!'

'No,' said Ms Legg, 'I certainly didn't.'

'Good!' said Leandra. 'We nearly exploded

having to keep it secret!'

'Keeping what secret?' asked Stacey, who wasn't really following. Leandra kicked her ankle.

'Ow!' she yelped.

'See?' said Leandra to Ms Legg. 'Brilliant!' She spotted William fighting his way through the crowd and grabbed him as he passed.

'Alexander!' she hissed. 'What's going on? Go and find out if your dad's still flipping his lid, will you?'

William glowed inside. That was twice in one evening he'd been mistaken for his friend Alexander. Edith aside, this really was shaping up to be a great Halloween.

'Yes, Leandra,' he said. He decided to try out one of those new-fangled words he was always hearing the others use. 'O-kay,' he said.

'And get on with it,' she hissed again. 'We can't keep them here all night.'

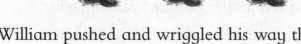

William pushed and wriggled his way through the crowd back towards the hall. This was no mean feat, as the corridor was heaving and most of the pupils were still heading towards the exit.

The hall, however, didn't have a single living being in it, although it was noisy all the same. It rang with the screechy sound of the Plague Pit Junior Ghost Band and the crowing of Edith Codd.

'Well, I showed them good and proper!' she cackled, rubbing her hands together so vigorously that great showers of skin flakes piled up on the floor around her feet. 'Did you see them? Did you? Running about like headless chickens! Squawking like them, too! They'll not be back here in a hurry, or my name's not Edith Codd!'

William was annoyed. *Silly hag*, he thought.

Always congratulating herself, and she never checks before she does it. Just because she's chased them out of here, she thinks she's got rid of them altogether. She really is more stupid than she looks!

He paused for a moment. *Which really is very stupid.*

The noise of the band combined with Edith's grating voice was so loud that she didn't hear William come up behind her. When he tapped her shoulder, she would have jumped out of her skin, had she still had one.

'You!' she shouted, glaring at the younger ghost. 'Don't think I've forgotten about you! Traitor! Numbskull!'

She took a swipe at his head.

William ducked. 'Before you congratulate yourself any more, Edith,' he said, 'I've got something to show you.'

'Oh, yes?' said Edith. 'What's that? Your yellow belly? Your forked tongue?'

'Come here,' he beckoned her towards the double doors, 'and see.'

Edith followed.

'Don't think I'm going to forget this, William Scroggins,' she was saying. 'Don't think you can just come crawling back and think it's all going to be forgotten. Things are going to be different from now on. You're going to . . . oh.'

They had reached the doors and William had swung them open. Edith, to her horror, was confronted with hundreds of pupils and teachers, all swigging blood, making jokes, being noisy and – curse it! – very much alive.

Edith was furious. She was seething. She had been made to look a fool in front of the plague-pit ghosts, and William was the reason it had happened.

She turned on him, her purple face clashing

horribly with her orange hair.

'You!' she shrieked, and spittle frothed out around her blackened teeth. 'It's always you! Well, that's it! No more! You horrid little upstart farmboy! I'll show you who's boss! I'll show you –'

She threw herself at William, but he was too fast. He shot across the dance floor, a howling Edith rushing in his wake. He dodged behind Bertram and used him as a shield, whizzing round to the other side every time Edith made a lunge.

'Quick!' he whispered. 'Play something.'

'Play what?' Bertram whispered back.

William had an idea. 'Play "Edith is a Loony"!' he hissed.

A big smile broke out on Bertram's face. 'Edith is a Loony' was his favourite of all the songs he had written over the centuries.

'Why, certainly!' he replied, raised his ribcage xylophone and struck the first note. The band,

recognising the tune in a moment, struck up in clashing harmony.

Edith stamped her foot. Her hair flew about her face and a shower of beetles sprayed from the nest behind her ear. 'Stop it!' she shrieked. 'Stop it, I say! You WILL NOT PLAY THAT SONG! I won't have it, do you hear?'

But the ghosts had already formed a conga line and were circling the hall, singing 'Edith is a loo-NY! Edith is a loo-NY!' at the tops of their voices.

Edith faced defeat. She wasn't powerful enough to overcome William, the ghost band and the entire company of the plague pit.

'I'll be back!' she shrieked. 'Don't think this is the last you've heard of Edith Codd!'

William threw open the double doors, and the conga line snaked out into the hall, the pupils and teachers of St Sebastian's School latching on as it passed.

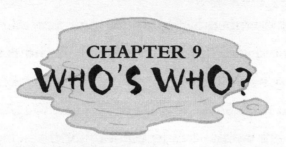

CHAPTER 9
WHO'S WHO?

Feeling the glow of a risky job well done, the boys went back towards the stairs leading to the school hall. James, particularly, felt relieved all round: not only had he saved St Sebastian's, but his stint as a DJ was well and truly over. He and Lenny chattered excitedly about their bravery.

'That was a close one!' said Lenny. 'I really thought she was going to get us this time!'

'Fwooar!' said James. 'I know. Did you smell her?'

'Yeah.' Lenny laughed. 'There's someone who

hasn't had a bath in a few hundred years!'

'Sort of – garlic and sweat,' observed James.

'Mixed with that pongy air freshener you get on dangly pine trees. And cheese. She honked of cheese.'

Only Alexander was quiet, lost in thought. James's mention of the pine tree air freshener had set off a worrying memory. His father had been given a large bottle of pine-scented aftershave for Christmas by the school secretary, Miss Keys, and, although it made him smell like the inside of a minicab and his mum wouldn't let it be opened in the house, he had taken to keeping it in his office beside the computer and splashing it on for special occasions. Could the St Sebastian's Halloween party have counted as a special occasion?

'I just wonder . . .' he began as they reached the bottom of the stairs.

James stopped. 'What's up, Stick?'

Alexander pulled one of his thinking faces. 'It's just . . .'

'Yes? Spit it out.'

'Well,' he continued, 'it's just that everyone knows that one of the primary phantasmagorical phenomena is the ability to transmogrify at a cellular level.'

James and Lenny stared at him.

'Or is it the other way round?' he pondered. 'I wonder. Is it perhaps that the phantasm can in some way alter the structure of solid matter it encounters, thereby rendering it in some way insubstantial? Fascinating. I'll have to do some research. Never mind. The fact remains that one of the better-known qualities of the incorporeal being is being unaffected by barriers.'

'In English?' James instructed.

'Oh. Sorry,' said Alexander. 'I was just wondering why our plan actually worked. Why we've got her trapped down there.'

'What do you mean?' asked Lenny.

'Well, everybody knows that ghosts can walk through walls,' replied Alexander. 'And doors.'

The three of them stopped and stared at each other uncomfortably.

'Oh,' said James.

'The thing is,' said Alexander, 'I have to say, even while we were running away, I couldn't help but notice that the thing sounded awfully like my father.'

'Oh,' said Lenny.

'Even under that ginger fright wig?' asked James.

Alexander nodded. 'And the thing is, I've never got the impression before that any of the ghosts had actually learnt our names.'

'Oh,' said James, again. 'Oh, dear.'

'But you *smelt* her breath,' said Lenny. 'You're not telling me a smell like that could come from a living being, are you?'

Alexander still looked doubtful. 'My dad's very fond of prawn curry,' he said. 'He had two helpings last night. With garlic pickle.'

James shook his head. 'Not even prawn curry could make a stench like that.'

Alexander was just considering mentioning the Gorgonzola sandwiches his mum had made for lunch when James's wizard beard was ruffled by a gust of freezing air.

'Watch out! Incoming!' shouted Lenny.

The three boys ducked as, with a plaintive scream, a flame-haired torpedo zipped over their heads and raced up the corridor.

'What was that?' shouted James, straightening his pointy wizard hat, which had been knocked sideways by the blast.

The smell that followed was inhuman: a rancid mix of fungus, rot, Camembert, unwashed hair, worms, burning plastic, sewage, BO, pig farms, mice and oranges that have been left in the bowl until their skins have turned green. And no, not a single whiff of pine-scented air freshener. It was so bad that even Lenny couldn't pretend that James had farted this time. There was only one place a smell like that could come from – and it was deep down, underneath the school.

The whirling, shrieking missile reached the door. Not pausing, even for a second, it vanished straight through it.

'Ah,' said Alexander. '*That* was what I was talking about.'

James looked at Alexander. Alexander looked at Lenny. Lenny looked at James. And between them, not one of them could think of anything to say.

The banging and shouting coming from the other side of the door suddenly stopped. For a moment, the only sound was the voice of Elvis

Presley, who was just beginning his eighth rendition that evening of 'Jailhouse Rock'.

The hammering started again. Accompanied by Mr Tick's unmistakable voice, panic-stricken. 'THIS ISN'T FUNNY ANY MORE! DO YOU HEAR ME? LET ME OUT! Alexander! James Simpson! Lenny Maxwell! Let me out NOW!'

The hammering turned, suddenly, into scuffling. The sound of Elvis was drowned out by the sound of Edith's scrawny cackle.

Lenny froze. He hardly dared imagine what might be going on on the other side of the door. Mr Tick would be no match for a furious witch, that was for sure – and if there was one thing that the mayhem up in the dance hall had convinced them of, it was that this was one furious witch.

Alexander, meanwhile, sprang into action. He ran down the corridor towards Mr Wharpley's cellar. That was his father locked in there, he was sure of it now, and nothing was going to stop him from rescuing him from that foul old look-a-like hag!

'Come on!' he shouted from the door. 'We can't leave him in there!'

James froze. Half of him wanted to conquer the ghost behind the door. The other half was more than aware that the only reason Mr Tick was locked in with her in the first place was because the three of them had tricked him in there. The thought of the wrath of Mr Tick on his release was very nearly as frightening as anything the supernatural world could unleash.

'Come *on*!' yelled Alexander. His normally pale face had turned an alarming shade of red. He had his hand on the key and was already pressing his shoulder to the door, ready to do battle.

'What are you *playing* at?' he bellowed. 'We've got to get him out!'

James and Lenny exchanged glances.

'We can't leave Stick to do this all by himself, you know,' said James.

'I know,' said Lenny.

'We'd better help, then,' said James.

'I guess we'd better,' said Lenny.

The two boys crept forwards to join their friend, hanging back behind him nervously as he struggled frantically with the lock.

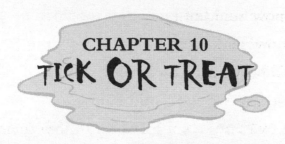

CHAPTER 10
TICK OR TREAT

Mr Tick's shouting gradually rose higher, until it blended in perfect harmony with Edith Codd's shrieks. Mr Tick no longer sounded like a headmaster. He didn't even sound like Alexander's father any more.

Alexander's hands were shaking, and his fingers had turned to sausages. The sound of his father's howls and yelps coming through the door were making him so nervous he might as well have been trying to grip the key with a full set of chipolatas. The shaking got worse as the roars got louder, until eventually he was trembling so much that he couldn't grip the key at all. He gazed pleadingly at James. He'd turned as green as Mrs Cooper's mushy peas.

'I can't do it,' he said. 'I can't open it.'

On the other side of the door, Mr Tick was having a very bad evening. It had started, he reflected, when he'd realised at precisely four o'clock that he had forgotten to hire a costume. It had worsened when he discovered that he'd left it so late that the only outfit left was this ridiculous witch's dress with its ginger wig and comedy teeth. It had careered downhill with the chaos in the hall. But the final straw had to be when his son – his *own son!* – and his friends had started hurling insults at him in the corridor and tripped him up into a pile of buckets. Some of which still contained water, he suspected, that had been used for mopping the boys' toilets.

And now he was locked in a smelly cellar with a frothing, stinking old hag who was dressed exactly like him! Obviously, it was some sort of practical joke, but he didn't see the funny side. In fact, he was finding the whole evening deeply disturbing.

'Detentions all round,' he muttered, and banged on the door again. 'This has gone too far.'

The hag eyed him from the corner of the room, over by the manhole leading down to the sewers. 'Haaah-ha-ha-ha-haaaa!' she cackled, and flexed a very convincing pair of clawed-finger gloves at him.

'Oh, do go away,' he said, longing for a cup of tea. 'Can't you see I'm busy?'

He raised his voice. 'James! Alexander! Leonardo! Open the door this instant! I'm warning you!'

'Lovely hair,' said Edith.

'Go away, woman!' he said commandingly.

'Lovely colour,' she said. Edith had always been extremely proud of her own ginger locks. As William always said, they matched her eyes. She grinned at the headmaster, giving him the full benefit of every blackened molar.

'Oh, do go away,' he repeated once more. The hag was more than irritating, he realised. He found her really quite scary.

'Gimme,' said Edith, and made a swipe at the headmaster's head.

Mr Tick turned round and folded his arms. 'Madam, I have to return this costume to the shop tomorrow. I certainly won't be giving you any part of it.'

'That's what *you* think!' shrieked Edith, and launched herself at him.

Mr Tick found himself in the middle of a whirlwind. A ghostly, cackling whirlwind that smelt of drains.

'It's mine!' shrieked Edith, making a grab at his head.

Mr Tick shrieked back.

'Nonononono!' he shouted. He wanted to run away, but there was nowhere to run to – and besides, his pesky skirt had wound itself round his legs, and kept him pinioned where he stood. Presuming that she was going for his eyes, he did the only thing he could think of. He covered his face with one hand and whirled the other arm round and round in the air, like a headmaster-shaped windmill.

'Gerroff!' he shrieked. Then, as his hand brushed through the slithery, greasy material of Edith's dress, his shriek rose a full octave.

'Yeeeuuuuggghhh!' he screamed. 'Get her off me! Get her off!'

Edith was having fun again after the humiliation upstairs. She cackled with excitement. A gust of stinking air hit his face.

Mr Tick stopped windmilling and clutched his nose and mouth with both hands. He stared into the eyes of Edith. This was the worst stench he had ever smelt. Worse than his mother's meatloaf. Worse than the time the dog had rolled in cow-dung. Worse than Paris, on a hot August

afternoon, in the middle of a dustmen's strike.

'Ha, HA!' cried Edith, triumphantly seizing the moment. She snatched the wig from his head and disappeared down the drain that led to the sewer.

The feeling James had had at the beginning of the disco had returned: the butterflies dancing around his stomach, the desire to turn tail and run. But he looked at his friend's stricken face and realised that he had to stand up and be counted.

'It's OK,' he said. 'I'll do it.'

He stepped past Alexander and put his hand on the key.

The lock was stiff, but after a few seconds the key caught and turned, and he tumbled through the door. The cellar was silent, apart from the strains of Elvis, glumly working his way through 'Are You Lonesome Tonight?'

Alexander stepped nervously forwards. 'Dad?'

he called. Lenny came forwards to stand beside
him.

'Dad?' called Alexander again.

There was a movement, in the shadows. The
three boys stiffened, unsure of what was going to
come out.

A figure shambled into the light. It was Mr Tick. His dress was torn and dirty and his face looked haggard. His wig, they noticed, was missing. He clutched Mr Wharpley's CD player to his chest, cradling it like a teddy bear.

'Dad?' said Alexander tentatively. 'Are you OK?'

'The "play" button's broken,' murmured Mr Tick. 'I don't seem to . . . and he won't stop singing . . .'

Alexander didn't say a word. Gently, he prised the machine from his father's hands and laid it down on Mr Wharpley's workbench. Elvis continued burbling about doorsteps and hearts as they slowly led the shattered headmaster up the stairs and to his office.

'It's OK, Dad,' Alexander said kindly, and helped his father to the chair behind his desk. Mr Tick put a thumb in his mouth and stared straight ahead, sucking.

Alexander pressed the 'on' button on Mr Tick's computer. The screen sprang into life. Already loaded was a half-played game of solitaire, green and familiar and soothing.

'Ah,' said Mr Tick vaguely, thumb still in his mouth. 'Black nine goes on red ten. I see it.'

He put his hand on the mouse and slowly began moving the cards about the screen. James, Alexander and Lenny quietly crept from the room and closed the door.

CHAPTER 11
THE MAGIC GLOWING BOX

William was the happiest ghost on the planet.
The conga line, which he had started ten
minutes ago, had grown so long that it had to
double back on itself three times to fit into the
hall. They had circled the hall twice to 'Edith is a
Loony' and twice more to Bertram's earliest
composition, 'A Niffy Nocturne'.

Now, as he got ready to lead the crowd out
through the double doors, along the corridor,
down the stairs and on a full circuit of the
school, the Plague Pit Junior Ghost Band

d tunes again, and struck up a rousing
of 'An Ode to Odour'. William cheered
loudly. This was his favourite of all of Bertram's
tunes. It seemed fitting that it should be playing
while he took his lap of honour.

He felt both happy and tired; staying solid *and*
dancing at the same time took a lot out of him.
William was in his element. Ghosts are meant to
have fun at Halloween, of course, but he'd never
had a Halloween as good as this one.

Stacey was happy, too. The party was the best-
attended and liveliest St Sebastian's had ever
seen! She didn't quite know how the school band
had managed to get their instruments out so
quickly when the CD player blew up – or how
they had managed to disguise them so well that
they really looked as though they were made of
bones – but they were a fantastic substitute for
the disco. Better, really, she reflected. James had
hardly managed to change a disc without some

mishap, and there was no way he'd have been able to actually lead a conga line any further than the flex would have stretched . . .

'Thank you so much,' she shouted, tugging on William's jerkin.

'What for?' shouted William.

'For, you know . . . everything,' shouted Stacey. 'Saving the day. We really appreciate it. Leandra and me. You know how much work we put into this thing, and we're very grateful.'

William glowed with pride. He stopped himself when he felt Stacey's grip loosen and realised that the glow had been on the *outside*. He looked over his shoulder to check that she hadn't noticed, and saw that her mouth was a round 'O' of surprise.

He smiled at her, encouragingly. *Just act normally*, he thought, *and maybe she'll think it was her eyes playing tricks*.

It worked. Stacey blinked a couple of times,

eyelashes batting up and down like a china
doll's, then grinned back. 'So did you manage to
calm him down, then?' she asked.

'Sorry?'

'Your dad. Sorry – Mr Tick. Did you manage
to get him under control? What did you do?'

William had forgotten that he was supposed to
be Alexander. He stammered as he struggled to
come up with an answer.

'Oh, uh, um, yes. Yes. It's all, um, er, fine, yes.'

'What did you do?' she asked. 'Lock him in a
cupboard?'

William was struggling to remember the
vocabulary of the modern world. He'd learnt
that James had been playing the music on things
called 'seedees', and that the horseless carriages
so many of the teachers came and went in were
called 'kaas', and that the little boxes the pupils
were always pressing to their ears and talking at
(and getting confiscated) were called 'mow-

byles', but he couldn't remember what the headmaster's favourite toy was called. The one on the desk in his office.

'No, it's fine,' he said, because he couldn't pause any longer, 'we left him playing on his magic glowing box.'

Stacey frowned. 'Magic glowing box?'

William nodded. 'Yes. You know. The one he keeps on his table. The one he stares at all day, muttering.'

Stacey was still frowning. She hadn't the first idea what Alexander was going on about. But then again, she seldom did.

The conga line had reached Miss Keys's office. The band were still playing with all their might, their bottoms waggling in time with their music.

'I don't . . .' began Stacey, and ran out of words when she saw something that didn't compute. James, Lenny and Alexander were letting themselves out through the door. 'Alexander!' she said. 'What on earth are you doing over there?'

Suddenly, she noticed that her hands no longer held on to anything and she was at the front of the line. Stacey blinked again, several times. How strange. She could have sworn that Alexander had been in front of her, but there he was, standing with his friends, getting ready to join on to the back of the chain.

Stacey shrugged. She was never one for worrying herself too much with things she didn't understand. 'Oh, well,' she said, and danced on down the corridor.

William had turned himself invisible the moment Stacey had clapped eyes on the real Alexander. A little bit of him had always known his fun couldn't go on forever.

'Ah, well,' he murmured as he passed the three boys in the doorway on his way to Mr Tick's private bathroom, 'it was fun while it lasted.'

James shivered as he passed. 'Did you hear that?' he asked Alexander.

'Hear what?' asked Alexander. He rubbed his upper arms briskly. It had turned cold, all of a sudden.

'I didn't hear anything,' said Lenny, 'but that pong's back again. You've not had another attack of nerves, have you, James?'

James elbowed him good-naturedly in the ribs. 'Come on,' he said, 'we might as well make the most of this band, wherever they've come from.'

William smiled wistfully. It had been great to share a night of fun with his friends, but now he had to face another, less attractive sort of music: the wrath of Edith Codd.

The bathroom off Mr Tick's office was the quickest route down to the sewers. William drifted forlornly past Miss Keys's desk, with its stuffed toy collection and pot of novelty pens, and peeped into Mr Tick's office through the small window in the door.

Mr Tick was sitting in front of the magic glowing box in his dress, mechanically moving the little box on wheels across the tabletop as he stared into the light. 'Black six on red seven,' he gurgled. 'Ah, look, the three's come free . . .'

William smiled. He might not be the *real* Alexander Tick, or ever really be able to be friends with him, but at least, it seemed, he knew how the boy's mind worked. The headmaster was doing exactly what William had told Stacey earlier.

'Black jack on red queen,' mumbled Mr Tick. 'That's the way to do it!'

CHAPTER 12
WHAT A PARTY!

'Now you mention it,' said James, 'that whiff's everywhere.'

'Yes,' said Lenny. 'Although I would swear it was stronger the closer I get to you.'

'Ha, ha,' said James. 'The one who smelt it, dealt it.'

'The one who denied it, supplied it,' rejoined Lenny.

'Didn't deny it,' said James.

Lenny pointed a sharp finger at him. 'So you *admit* it then!'

James rolled his eyes. The smell was very strong. A horde of plague-pit ghosts in a conga line is one of the smelliest things on the planet. Each ghost had his or her own peculiar aroma, which blended together to make a stench of mythical proportions. Old broccoli, swimming towels left in a plastic bag, Brie, pigeon droppings, dustbins, drains, onions, Brussels sprouts, diesel: these were just a few of the choice scents.

The Plague Pit Junior Ghost Band played 'The Supernatural Salsa' and the crowd, with a smiling Stacey at the front and a grinning Leandra behind her, conga'd back towards the hall.

'Well, they all seem to be having fun, anyway,' observed Alexander.

'Shall we join in?'

They latched on to the end of the line as it kicked its way past. James found himself holding on to the corduroy jacket of Mr Hall, the history teacher. Mr Hall jumped in the air and clapped his suede brogues together every time the music paused. It was quite hard to hold on.

Everyone was puffing and panting by the time they reached the hall. Stacey, Leandra, Mrs Cooper and Mrs Meadows poured and handed out cups of blood and the pupils fell on what was left of the buffet. The ghosts, however, were still full of energy, Lady Grimes in particular. Her husband had been very strict during her lifetime, and she had been determined to make up for it ever since. It wasn't long before she had organised the entire room into ranks for a line-dance.

Pupils, teachers and ghosts all stood in rows waiting to hear what tune the Band was going to treat them to. The 'Phantom Polka', perhaps? Or the tricky 'Drain Dance'?

Everyone sighed with relief when they struck up with Bertram's bumptious Country and

Western tribute, 'Achy Breaky Fart'. He had heard the original song when Mr Wharpley had accidentally brought one of his wife's CDs into work rather than his favourite Elvis album.

'I know this!' shouted James over the racket of thigh-bone trombones and sinus kazoos.

'Even I know it!' replied Alexander.

The whole company threw themselves vigorously into the dance: left, right, kick, clap, turn. Everyone agreed that this was the best party St Sebastian's School had ever seen!

It was so much fun, in fact, that not one of the pupils had the time to be embarrassed by their teachers' dancing. And some of it was very embarrassing indeed. A teacher dancing is not a pretty sight. As everybody knows, teachers have their sense of rhythm surgically removed at college. The hall was a sea of wobbly tummies and flapping elbows. Mr Parker and Ms Legg were doing a clumsy jive.

'I just hope,' bellowed James, 'he doesn't try to throw her over his head. He'll be in traction for months!'

Mr Downe had undone the top button of his shirt to show off a large gold medallion. His chest, they noticed, was a great deal hairier than his head. He was throwing disco moves that hadn't been seen since the 1970s, his finger poking the air above his head.

Lenny nudged James and nodded at him. 'What does he look like!' he shouted. James was having too much fun himself to point out that Lenny's own hands were so large and his arms so gangly that he looked like he was waving a pair of soup plates around. 'Never mind Mr Downe,' he shouted back. 'Mr Wharpley looks like he needs the loo!'

They both stared at the caretaker, who had found his Elvis wig again and clamped it back on to his head. He was in the middle of the dance floor, knees clamped together and upper lip curled so hard it looked like he was holding it up with a coat-hanger, strutting up and down. The occasional 'thngyouvrrymuch' escaped his mouth.

'He does, doesn't he?' yelled Alexander. 'The fact that that catsuit hasn't split yet is an anomaly unexplained by quantum physics.'

All too soon, the dance was over, and the
Plague Pit Junior Ghost Band, after a brief
conference with Ambrose, started up with a
down-tempo number, the 'Whiffy Waltz'.
Ambrose stalked across the dance floor, bowed
deep and offered his hand to Lady Grimes. She
cooled herself with a fan made of fish-bones and

took it. Soon, the pair was floating across the dance floor, a couple of inches in the air.

Eyes shining, Stacey tapped Alexander on the shoulder.

'How about a thank-you dance?' she asked. She still hadn't put two and two together about the 'other' Alexander she'd been conga-ing with in the corridor. Stacey tended to assume, if she didn't understand something, that she had just made a mistake. It had to have been Alexander she'd been talking to, didn't it?

Alexander blushed to the roots of his hair. He had no idea what Stacey was thanking him for, but he wasn't going to embarrass himself more by asking. 'Of course,' he said.

They stepped on to the floor and set off, and Alexander racked his brain for something to talk about.

'Oh, I know,' he said. 'Did you hear the one about the two chimps in the bath?'

'No,' said Stacey, looking up at him with her big blue eyes.

'The first chimp went "Ooh-ooh-ooh-ooh-ah-ah-ah-ah,"' said Alexander, 'and the second one said, "Well, put some more cold in, then."'

Stacey looked blank. 'I didn't know chimps could talk,' she said.

James was a bit miffed. After his noble efforts at DJ-ing, he felt the least he deserved was a dance with Stacey. Still, he wasn't going to show it. He noticed Leandra standing nearby, looking hopeful, and tapped her on the shoulder.

'Dance?' he shouted.

Leandra thought about it for about two seconds. She was still supposed to be cross about the CD player. Then she shrugged and let bygones be bygones. Though she decided that she'd get her own back by treading on his toes.

118

Lenny heaved a sigh of relief: he was off the hook. All the girls were partnered up by now and he had the full run of the buffet. His pet rat, Whiskers, he discovered, liked the flaky cheese fingernails on the bubonic fingers – a lot.

'A good night all round,' he said to the rodent, and took a swig from a cup someone had left lying on the table. It tasted strangely salty, and was thicker than a normal drink, a bit like cream. He looked down and saw something floating in it that looked suspiciously like a leech.

Lenny hurriedly put the cup down and edged away from the table.

CHAPTER 13
MILK AND TWO SUGARS

The only person at the party who wasn't dancing was Miss Keys. Now she knew that the incident in the hall had been forgotten, all she could really think about was making sure that he was all right. *Such a nice man, such a good headmaster. Such a shame that he was under all this pressure . . .*

While Lenny was edging away from Ambrose's forgotten cup of leech wine, she edged towards the door. She would just go and check, she thought. Just make sure.

The light was on in her office, but Mr Tick's room was dark. Miss Keys called softly through the door.

'Hello?'

There was no answer. But Miss Keys could see an eerie, greenish glow. His computer was on. Mr Tick never left his office without switching his computer off. She knew he was in there.

She popped her handbag on to her desk and, chatting so he knew she was there, she got out the keys to her drawers.

'It's turning out to be a lovely evening,' she said. Mr Tick didn't reply. 'Everyone's dancing and enjoying themselves, you don't have to worry.'

She kept a value-pack of chocolate biscuits in her bottom drawer, for special occasions. Still in her vampire cape, Miss Keys bent over and took them out. Then she filled the kettle and flicked the switch.

'I saw your son dancing with that nice Stacey Carmichael,' she continued, arranging the biscuits on a plate. 'Goodness, how quickly they grow up! Pink in the face, he was.'

She heard a slight movement in the darkened office. A soft voice muttered something about aces being low. *That's better*, she thought. *He knows I'm here. A nice cup of tea will sort him out, and I know just how he likes it.*

She picked Mr Tick's 'Solitaire Champ' mug off the draining board and put two teabags in. *Good and strong*, she thought. *That'll help.*

'And you should have seen Mr Wharpley!' she chuckled. 'He was wiggling about like he'd got ants in his pants!'

'Black three on red four,' replied Mr Tick.

Miss Keys added milk and two sugars to the tea, and put the mug and the plate of biscuits on a tray. She flicked back her cape and carried the refreshments through to the headmaster's office,

pushing the door open with her bottom.

'There you go,' she said chirpily, putting it down beside him. 'Never mind. A nice cup of tea, and everything will be fine, don't you worry ...'

Meanwhile, William was squeezing himself through a pipe and into the slimy place he called home. Even down in the sewer, the sound of the disco was deafening. The music bounced off the walls as though it were alive.

Edith will want my guts for garters, he thought mournfully. *And this racket isn't going to put her in a better mood.*

William had had a fantastic night, a night he would remember for a long, long time. Not only had he danced with Stacey, he'd laughed and conga'd and been mistaken several times for Alexander and, best of all, he'd saved the entire night. It didn't matter that no one – well, no one apart from Edith – knew that he'd done it: the fact that he'd had such an important part in such a successful party made everything worth it.

Everything. Even the wrath of Codd.

Knowing that he couldn't avoid her forever, William crept nervously into the amphitheatre.

If anything, the noise was louder here. The amphitheatre was designed to produce an echo –

so Edith's scratchy voice would carry to every corner – and it was amplifying the sound from upstairs like a loudspeaker. William could hear the noise of stamping feet and laughter, and even make out the sounds of the Junior Ghost Band's individual instruments: the rootle-toot of a wristbone flute and the boom-boom-boom of a drum.

She'll be going bonkers, he thought. *I'm really in for it.*

He hid in the shadows. He hardly dared open his eyes. *OK, here goes,* he decided, and slid from the darkness to meet his fate.

What he saw made his eyes very nearly fall out. Because far from ranting and raving and plotting revenge, Edith was dancing!

Her carroty hair whirled around in the air, followed by the carroty hair of her partner. William had to squint to see what was going on, and when he did he started back in surprise.

Edith was not only dancing, she was smiling so widely that every one of her green and blackened teeth was showing. And her partner was grinning equally widely – but that was hardly surprising, since it was a skeleton. She'd obviously picked it out from the pile of bones which made up the amphitheatre's seating and, from somewhere, she'd found a red wig to plonk on its bleached skull.

'What a pair we make,' trilled Edith as she whirled her silent partner round the floor. 'Don't we?'

With a scabby hand, Edith released her grip on the skeleton's bony shoulder and reached up to hold the skull. With a grinding of bones and a small burst of dust, Edith's hand helped the skeleton to nod enthusiastically.

'Indeed we do, Edith,' croaked the skeleton, in the voice of Edith Codd. 'And may I say how fine you're looking this evening? Elegant, though

I say it myself.'

'Why, thank you, Edith,' squawked Edith.
'You're too kind! What is it about me? My dress?
My hair?'

'Why, all of it,' croaked the skeleton. 'Every last
morsel. But the best thing of all is your simple
magnificence.'

Edith simpered. She looked a bit like a frog

127

swallowing an over-large fly.

'You were magnificent tonight, Edith!' croaked Edith, in the skeleton voice. 'Magnificent! You had them on the run, and they'll never forget it.'

'Do you really think so, Edith?'

'Absolutely, Edith.'

'Well, I'm glad you think so, Edith,' grated Edith. 'I'll finish them off properly next time, of course.'

'Of course you will, Edith,' assured the skeleton. 'Of course you will.'

'Well, I'll be jiggered,' thought William, and suddenly realised he'd said it out loud. He glanced nervously at Edith, but she was too absorbed in dancing with herself to even look up.

He'd had a lucky escape. Before his luck ran out, William crept quietly back the way he had come. If he hurried, there was probably time for one more dance.

SURNAME: Maxwell

FIRST NAME: Leandra

AGE: 13

HEIGHT: 1.7 metres

EYES: Brown

HAIR: Black

LIKES: Football; athletics; running about; in fact, anything vaguely sporty, especially if it involves beating boys at their own game!

DISLIKES: The colour pink; anything fluffy; pop music; anything too girly (she leaves all of that stuff to best friend Stacey Carmichael)

SPECIAL SKILL: Sticking up for her little brother Lenny - even though he doesn't always want her help!

INTERESTING FACT: Leandra has an incredible ability to talk her way out of sticky situations. Unlike her bro, Leandra is frequently in trouble at school - but somehow she always manages to win the teachers over. In fact, her big mouth gets her out of as much trouble as it gets her into!

For more facts on Leandra Maxwell, go to **www.too-ghoul.com**

Alexander Tick's
Joke File

(page 4,812)

Q What flower grows between your nose and your chin?

A Two-lips!

Q Why do cows wear bells?

A Because their horns don't work!

Q Where do you find a one-legged dog?

A Where you left it!

Q What's the chilliest football ground in England?

A Cold Trafford!

NOTE TO SELF: input these into jokes database at earliest convenience

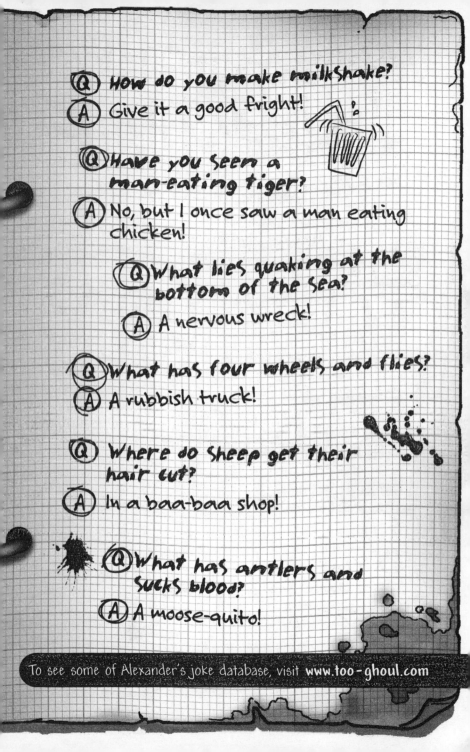

Q How do you make milkshake?
A Give it a good fright!

Q Have you seen a man-eating tiger?
A No, but I once saw a man eating chicken!

Q What lies quaking at the bottom of the sea?
A A nervous wreck!

Q What has four wheels and flies?
A A rubbish truck!

Q Where do sheep get their hair cut?
A In a baa-baa shop!

Q What has antlers and sucks blood?
A A moose-quito!

Make Your Own
Halloween

See if your own spooky dinner attracts a
bunch of fearsome ghouls to the table . . .
and we don't mean your family, either!

Worm Jelly

Ask a grown-up to help you
mix up half a packet of green
jelly and pour it into a large
bowl. When it's set, sprinkle
on jelly-worm sweets. Then mix
up the other half of the packet,
pour over the top, and put it in the
fridge. Sprinkle on some long shoelace
sweets for added wormy effect!

Severed Fingers

Ask a grown-up to help you
cut some thin, nail-shaped
slices of cheese. Stick
them on to the ends of
frankfurters using
ketchup or mustard, and
arrange five to a plate in
a hand shape.

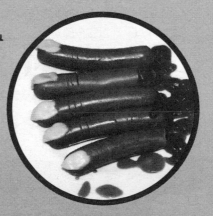

Feast

Worm Burgers

Ask a grown-up to help you cut some burger buns in half and to open a tin of spaghetti. Lay the bun bases out in a row and dollop a big spoonful of spaghetti on to each. Make sure it drips over the sides! Squish on the bun tops so the worms ooze out!

Severed-Hand Lollies

Ask a grown-up to help you fill some clean rubber gloves with blackcurrant squash. Tie the ends tightly and freeze them. When they're solid, pull the gloves off and float them in a bowl of fruit punch. Yuck!

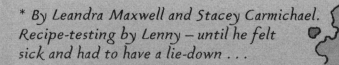

By Leandra Maxwell and Stacey Carmichael. Recipe-testing by Lenny — until he felt sick and had to have a lie-down . . .

Plague Pit Junior
Ghost Band Song Sheet

Conductor and Xylophone Soloist: B. Ruttle

Stop skin flaking over music sheets during solo →

'Plague Victims' March'
With hollowed-out leg-bone solo by Jim Scroat

'I've Got A Lovely Bunch Of Skulls'
Rib-bone xylophone solo by B. Ruttle

'How Much Is That Zombie In The Window?'
Rotting-arm lute duet, featuring
Fingers McGrott and Eileen Sludge

Don't tap foot during quiet bit: toes rattling drown out music →

'Dance In B Sharp'
By P. Cutlass, plague-pit swordsman

'Oh, I Do Like To Be Beside The Grave Side!'
(Croak-along with plague-pit choir)

'My Old Man's A Dust-Ghoul'
With coffin-lid drum solo by B. Shaker

'March In A Flat Minor'
Squashed-horn solo by a very flat miner

'Ode To Odour'
Composed specially by B. Ruttle

Remember to tune up leg-bones for this one ←

Can't wait for the next book in the series?
Here's a sneak preview of

STAGE FRIGHT

available now from all good bookshops,
or **www.too-ghoul.com**

CHAPTER 1
ROMEO AND GHOULIET

'Out the way! Coming through!'

James Simpson dropped his school bag and barged his way to the front of the crowd. Lenny Maxwell was already there, staring at a poster stuck to the St Sebastian's School noticeboard.

'What's going on?' James asked his friend. 'They're not holding another custard-eating contest are they? I spent three days on the toilet after the last one!'

Lenny shook his head. 'Nah. Nothing as exciting as that,' he grunted. 'They're putting on a school play. I don't fancy it much myself – sounds too much like hard work!'

James studied the poster. It was fixed to the rotting noticeboard with a bit of old chewing gum. 'WANTED!' it said in big letters. 'ACTORS TO STAR IN ROMEO AND GHOULIET! SIGN UP HERE!'

'Yeah. Sounds duller than one of Mr Tick's assemblies,' James agreed.

'And what's worse, we'd have to miss science lessons to go to rehearsals!' said a voice behind them.

Alexander Tick squeezed through the chattering crowd and peered at his best friends over a huge pile of textbooks.

'Did you say we get to miss science lessons, Alexander?' Lenny asked, raising his eyebrows.

'Yes – terrible, isn't it?' Alexander replied. 'Imagine – what kind of idiot would want to do a stupid school play instead of learning about the magic of science with Mr Watts? Why, you'd have to be some kind of . . . James? What are you doing?'

James had grabbed a pen from Alexander's blazer pocket and was frantically scribbling his name on the sign-up sheet.

'Missing science?' he cried. 'Count me in!'

Lenny snatched the pen off him and added his name to the list.

'Too right, mate!' he nodded. 'I'd sign up to be a ballet dancer if it meant getting out of Mr Watt's weekly boring-o-thon!'

Alexander scowled at them both.

'All I can say is Mr Watts has more talent in his little finger than any of those rubbish footballers you like so much!'

Lenny rolled his eyes. 'I know the headmaster's son is meant to be a nerd, Stick,' he groaned. 'But you really take your duties too far!'

James peered at the small print on the poster. 'Yeah – and they need a lighting engineer for the play, too. Why don't you sign up?'

'Lighting engineer?' said Alexander, his ears pricking up. 'I suppose that would be a rather interesting project! I could investigate the effect of rewiring the stage lights with improved resistors. But what about Mr Watts?'

James grabbed the pen and wrote Alexander's name on the list.

'Oh, come on, Stick!' he laughed. 'You spend every weekend reading about science. You spend every lunchtime boring us about it. And Lenny and I are still mentally scarred from the science-themed birthday party you made us go to. So missing a few lessons won't do you any harm!'

'Hey – the effects of that chemical wore off after a week,' said Alexander. 'Anyway, I've got to go. The Gorilla is making me do his maths homework for him!'

'Shhhh!' hissed James with a frown.

'What?' cried Alexander. 'That big oaf is too stupid to do it himself, so he bullies me into it. I'm going to put the wrong answers down, anyway!'

Lenny kicked Alexander on the shin. 'Shut up, you idiot!'

'Oh, don't tell me you're scared!' Alexander continued. 'That meat-head will never find out.

He might be a brute, but he's got a brain the size of a p-p-p . . .'

Alexander tailed off. James and Lenny were staring over his shoulder.

'H–h–he's behind me, isn't he?' Alexander whimpered. A fierce punch to the back of his head confirmed his theory.

'Owwwww!'

'If I didn't need my maths homework by lunchtime, I'd squash you for that!' Gordon 'The Gorilla' Carver grunted. 'Now do it!'

Alexander scurried off while Gordon wrinkled up his nose and peered at the noticeboard.

'Right!' he boomed. 'What about this play, then?'

James looked surprised. 'I didn't have you down as an actor, Gordon!' he said nervously.

The bully scowled at him and snatched the pen from his hand.

'Shut it, squirt!' he muttered. 'Anything to get

142

out of lessons! And I hear there's fighting in it. Proper fighting!'

He thumped his huge fist against the noticeboard, which wobbled off its rotten frame and came crashing down on to Lenny's toe.

'This school is the pits!' James grumbled.

'Tell me about it!' Lenny agreed. 'If it doesn't get sorted out soon, they'll have to add hard-hats to the uniform!

'Hello, Mr Tick speaking. How can I help?'

The headmaster yawned down the phone and fiddled with his 'Best Headmaster in the World' mug.

'Uh-huh. You're an ex-pupil. How interesting.'

He yawned again and picked up his computer mouse, absent-mindedly moving playing cards about on the screen. He hated phone calls – they disturbed his solitaire practice.

'Well, we don't normally allow visits to the school from ex-pupils, I'm afraid . . .' he said grumpily. 'Now if there's nothing else . . .'

But he froze halfway through hanging up.

'What? A donation to the school? How much?' he cried. 'W-w-well maybe I was a bit hasty. Of course you can visit the school, Lord Goldsworthy. Why not come down and see our school play? And we can talk some more about this donation!'

He was still punching the air when Miss Keys, the school secretary, burst into his office.

'Mr Tick! It's the PE block!' she cried hysterically. 'The roof has blown clean off!'

Mr Tick frowned. 'What do you want me to do about it?' he grumbled, his hand moving back down to his mouse.

'But the children are getting drenched in the rain!' the secretary wailed. 'One of the classrooms is filling with water!'

144

Mr Tick glanced out of the window at the PE block. The roof was over in the playing field. Some frightened, damp faces were pressed up against one of the rotten windows.

'Then send them over some armbands from the swimming pool!' tutted the headmaster. 'I'm not made of money, you know!'

As Miss Keys shuffled meekly out, he grabbed a pencil and a piece of paper.

'PLANS FOR LORD GOLDSWORTHY'S MONEY,' he wrote in big letters at the top of the page.

'No. 1: NEW HEADMASTER'S OFFICE.'

He sat back and admired his list. 'Yes. That's what this school needs!' he smiled. 'A new building – for the best headmaster in the world!'

Mr Tick's voice echoed around his office, down the pipes in the corner, and into a dark, slimy pit deep under the school. In a corner of this pit, pressing her ear to the rusty pipe, was a disgusting old hag with flaky, rotting skin, fuzzy hair and bony witch's fingers. She let out a horrid, rasping groan.

'A new building?' the hag screeched. 'That'll mean even more noise from that pesky school!'

She put her pasty, peeling ear to the pipe again.

'I'll show them, though!' she cackled. 'No one messes with Edith Codd!'